Cassius C. Cullen

The American melodies, in three parts, and miscellaneous poems

Part I. - III.

Cassius C. Cullen

The American melodies, in three parts, and miscellaneous poems
Part I. - III.

ISBN/EAN: 9783743335226

Manufactured in Europe, USA, Canada, Australia, Japa

Cover: Foto ©Andreas Hilbeck / pixelio.de

Manufactured and distributed by brebook publishing software
(www.brebook.com)

Cassius C. Cullen

The American melodies, in three parts, and miscellaneous poems

THE

AMERICAN MELODIES,

IN THREE PARTS,

AND

MISCELLANEOUS POEMS,

BY

CASSIUS C. CULLEN.

———

TRENTON, N. J.
MURPHY & BECHTEL, PRINTERS, OPPOSITE CITY HALL.
———
1864.

TO THE

GALLANT AND PATRIOTIC

SOLDIERS OF NEW JERSEY, AS A

SLIGHT TRIBUTE TO THEIR HEROIC CONDUCT,

UNFLINCHING GALLANTRY AND INVINCIBLE COURAGE,

WHICH HAS BEEN TESTED ON MANY A HARD-FOUGHT, BLOOD-

STAINED BATTEFIELD OF OUR COUNTRY, IN DEFENCE OF

OUR HOMES AND FIRESIDES, AND THE PRE-

SERVATION OF OUR GLORIOUS UNION,

THESE MELODIES ARE RES-

PECTFULLY INSCRIBED

BY THE

AUTHOR.

PREFACE.

In presenting these Melodies to the American public, I have no apologies to make, nor favors to ask. They were written from time to time, as my feelings moved me or the muse inspired me. I neither was actuated by any desire for literary celebrity or love of fame. Little did I imagine, in the composition of the Melodies which constitute the first part, that they would ever meet with publication; but after having written quite a large number, I have succumbed to the desire of a few friends, and consigned them to the press.

I have constantly endeavored throughout the preparation of this work to strictly adhere to my original intention of making it American in tone and sentiment. How far I have succeeded in this the public may judge. Indeed, I have met with but little stimulation to induce me to sing the glories of a foreign land. Our own American forests, in all their primitive grandeur and sublimity, present to any lover of nature such exquisitely picturesque scenery that neither Europe nor Asia can furnish their comparison.

Where can be found more noble streams than the "lordly Mississippi," the queenly Ohio, or the graceful Hudson. whose banks present unrivalled scenery for observation and study.

Whatever sparks of genius these Melodies may possess, they can never be attributed to my scholastic attainments or literary merit. They are but the offspring of imagination or the productions of creative fancy, warmed into poetic life by an ardent love of the beautiful and sublime in nature, which all mankind possess to a greater or less extent, requiring but a small degree of cultivation preparatory to its existence in verse.

Owing to the large class of lyrical writers who have preceded me, it may justly be inquired: Do these Melodies possess any originality of thought, or freshly-created conceptions? To this interrogatory I might truly reply that, to my present knowledge, there is nothing which this work contains that has in any wise been extracted from the productions of another author, save a few quotations which have been inserted for the sake of embellishment, and for which the authors are duly accredited.

Byron, in a preface to one of his poems, loudly complains of the difficulty of producing anything original, ascribing as a reason the voluminous effusions of preceding poets—and no doubt he uttered the truth.

Allen Ramsay, a Scotch poet of some known celebrity, who preceded him by about half a century, in the preface to his works, made use of the following significant language:—" Throughout the whole I have only copied from nature; and, with all precaution, have studied, as far as it came within the ken of my observation and memory, not to repeat what has already been said by others, though it be next to impossible sometimes to stand clear of them, especially in the little love plots of a song."

Here, then, is a writer who flourished in the beginning of the eighteenth century, when lyrical composition was almost in its infancy, building up the same plea as his more illustrious compeer. If a writer living in that early age appeals to the public for a justification of what may be styled a repetition of other author's productions, it may well be inquired what cause have I for the same. Since the days of Ramsay a numerous class of lyrical poets have flourished, as well as epic, which leaves it still more difficult to avoid stumbling upon any of their productions. Thomas Moore, who is perhaps one of the most voluminous of English song composers has his fame nearly, if not entirely, founded upon his melodies; and the same might be applied to Burns. Sir Walter Scott has left behind him various specimens in this style of composition.

I might proceed still further, and enumerate others of the same kinddred; but let those suffice. I furnish these illustrations merely as a basis upon which to erect my justification, provided there may be found in my writings a single thought or simile justly belonging to another author.

With these few remarks, I submit these Melodies to the learned world, conscious of the many imperfections they may contain, yet basing my vindication on the ground that they were published at the desire of a few friends, and with little or no preparation for the press.

THE
AMERICAN MELODIES.

PART I.

CONSISTING OF A NUMBER OF ORIGINAL AMERICAN MELODIES,
COMPOSED BEHIND THE PLOW PRIOR TO THE
WAR FOR THE UNION.

"How dear to this heart are the scenes of my childhood,
When fond recollection presents them to view;
The orchard, the meadow, the deep-tangled wildwood,
And ev'ry loved spot which my infancy knew."
—SAMUEL WADSWORTH.

WAR SONG.

Americans, your fathers dead
Call from their glorious, honored bed,
And point to rivers running red,
   All gory with their blood.

And do you hear their warning voice?
O, ye! their hope, their pride, their choice!
They tell you of the costly price
   Of your own Liberty.

Behold upon your soil the slaves!
And will you view them there, ye braves,
To tread your fathers' holy graves
   'Neath their unhallowed feet?

No! by our God who reigns above!
No! by our freedom which we love!
No! by our swords whose steel shall prove,
   They'll never touch this soil.

For sacred is each blood-dyed plain;
Where they were murdered, they were slain,
And long as blood shall course a vein,
   We will protect each tomb.

Since they for us did willing die,
Then who could their last wish deny—
To shield their dust where it doth lie,
   Or perish by its side?

Long as the Rocky Mountains stand,
Or Mississippi's waters grand
Flow through our broad and stretching land,
    Their holy graves are ours.

How dare they land upon our sod,
Made sacred to none but our God,
Do they expect we'll bear their rod,
    And meekly be chained down ?

No, never ! may our watchword be,
Give us Death or Liberty !
For who could live, and not be free,
    Chained to their cursed yoke?

Then sleep, our fathers ! no vile slave
Shall crawl across one sacred grave,
While guarded by your sons so brave,
    The sons of Liberty.

For every rod we will dispute,
Till we from us the oppressors root ;
Before they'll gain one inch, one foot,
    They'll wade through seas of blood.

STUNG BY REMORSE, WE OFT LOOK BACK.

Stung by remorse, we oft look back,
    On days we idly let pass by,
And wish that we could live them o'er,
    A better course of life to try.
But what is past, is past and gone,
    And never will return again ;
Improve the present while it's thine,
    Or we may view e'en it with pain,

ON WASHINGTON.

"The Father of his Country."
"First in War, first in Peace, and first in the Hearts of his Countrymen."

"O wake not the hero, his battles are o'er,
Let him rest undisturbed by Potomac's fair shore;
By the river's green border so flowery drest,
With the hearts he loved fondly, let Washington rest."

How fair does roll the placid wave
Which beats hard by the hero's grave!
How lovely are the banks below,
Which skirt the waters as they flow,
While moving on their flow'ry way,
Seem loth to meet the briny bay.
Such is the stream that rolls so sweet,
Beneath the hero-patriot's feet;
'Tis seen from rise to set of sun,
That tomb—the grave of Washington!

Rest, noble Chief! and may the fires
Inspire the sons which flamed their sires;
So, when disunion draws the blade,
No dreader watchword need be made,
To drive those fiends to terror—shame—
Than sound abroad thy glorious name.
Then would Columbia's millions rise,
To shield each hero where he lies;
'Twould strike those traitors trembling dumb,
Would thy great name, our Washington!

Thy name shall live till time will cease,
A household word through war and peace,
A rallying sound for freedom's band,
The watchword of your native land;

The pride of children yet unborn,
The brilliant sun of freedom's morn,
Who led the road and trod-the path
That leads to "liberty or death!"
Whose grateful land through time to come,
Will boast the name of Washington!

DEAR LAND OF MY FATHERS, WITH WHAT FOND ENDEARMENTS.

Dear land of my fathers, with what fond endearments,
  Afar o'er the ocean, in some foreign clime,
My heart swells with rapture, my soul with emotion,
  As proudly I claim that Columbia is mine.

Her mem'ry unfading shall dwell in my bosom,
  While nobly I'll boast of the land of the free;
As I stray on the banks of the Seine or the Danube,
  I'll love thee more dear, though far distant from me.

Alone I may stray by the wandering Niger,*
  Alone I may sit on the banks of the Nile;†
But still, though the distance grow wider between us,
  More fondly I'll love thee at each length'ning mile.

I may tread the turf by the shore of the Ganges,‡
  And feast with delight in the cool orange grove,
May bathe in the breeze of an Indian summer,
  But can I forget thee, dear land of my love?

---

*The largest navigable stream in Africa; the source of which was a matter of considerable comment among the ancients.
†The much celebrated river of Egypt.
‡The idolized stream of Hindoostan.

O no; though I dwell in the cold Polar regions,
  Or roam or reside in the hot Torrid zone,
E'en then will I think on thee, land of my fathers,
  And drop a sad tear for my country, my home.

O DEAR, HONORED DAY.*

Independence now, and independence forever.—DANIEL WEBSTER.

TUNE—"*The American Star.*"

O, dear honored day, how I feel the emotion
  Arise in my bosom when thinking on thee;
I turn with affection, the warmest devotion,
  To honor those martyrs who gave thee to me.

But where are those martyrs, my country's great glory?
  Where's Livingston, Adams, her Jefferson gone?
Emblazoned their mem'ry shall circle in story,
  Their fame lives behind them, though set is their sun.

Our Washington slumbers, and ne'er shall awaken,
  To lead freedom's brave sons to victory on;
His mem'ry is sacred whose soul stood unshaken,
  Through lust of ambition for the cause he had won.

Farewell, then, ye heroes; for long as in mourning
  Your country the loss of her pride shall deplore,
For when treason was rife, and its dark tempest lowering,
  Stood constant and firm to the cause which ye bore.

---

*The above stanzas were composed for the 4th of July, 1860, on the
summit of a lofty eminence overlooking West Point, on the Hudson, the
seat of the United States Military Academy, on the road from Fishkill to
Cold Spring.

Then rest ye yourselves while your country keeps weeping,
And Columbia's tears fall to moisten the sod;
They'll value the prize you have left to their keeping,
And bow down the knee to no king but their God.

BANKS OF CHAMPLAIN.*

I have roamed the east, I've roamed the west,
   I have roamed from Florida to Maine;
O, recall me now to take my rest,
   On the lovely banks of sweet Champlain.

I have stood by Mississippi's shore,
   And the broad Missouri stream in vain,
For to find a place that I'd love more,
   Than the lovely banks of fair Champlain.

I have climbed the Rocky Mountains high,
   And have stood beside the Western main;
But no place so charming could I view,
   As the lovely banks of dear Champlain.

I have been on England's fruitful soil,
   And reviewed the sunny land of Spain;
O, then call me from my rambling toil,
   To the lovely banks of calm Champlain.

No; I have roamed the world all round,
   Nor shall I wish to roam again—
I am well content; no place I've found,
   Like the lovely banks of sweet Champlain.

*Composed sitting on the shore of Lake Champlain, at the beautiful town of Burlington, in the State of Vermont, in September, 1858.

BEHOLD THE PROUD FREEMAN BY HIS LOVELY OHIO.*

Behold the proud freeman by his lovely Ohio!
    He roams unafraid, for he knows that he's free;
He asks but his freedom, with peace and contentment,
    To monarchs or tyrants he won't bend the knee.

How fair are the banks of the great Yang-tse-ki-ang,†
    Where pineapples flourish and citron trees wave!
But tell me who're those that rejoice by its waters—
    Are they not the foot-stool of tyrants, the slave?

The slaves may rejoice in their groves of sweet oranges;
    Of Cashmere and Ganges‡ exultantly boast;
They may sit in the shade of the palm and the olive—
    Delight in the fruit of their coral-bound coast.

Away with such splendors, that dazzle and brighten,
    But give me a home by Ohio so dear;
It's there let me ramble, it's there let me wander,
    Where tyrants might quake and kings tremble with fear.

---

*Composed while a resident of Lawrence county, Ohio, on the banks of the above named stream.

†A noble river of China; next in length to the Mississippi, and called by the Chinese "Mother of Waters."

‡A famous valley and river in India; the former the poet Moore has immortalized in verse.

O! GIVE ME MY HOME IN THE WEST!

Tune—"*There's a Spot that I Love.*"

I have wandered where luxury revels with pride,
    Where pleasure has made man her slave;
With reluctance I've tasted her follies, and sighed
    For my home where the forest trees wave.

O, give me the hum of the wild, busy bee,
And the song of the robin-red-breast;
O, give me the shade of the spreading beech tree—
O, give me my home in the West.

How dear to this heart is each verdant retreat,
Those groves of old sycamore trees,
Beneath whose huge branches I've gazed at the wheat
As it swayed in the breath of the breeze;
And happy is he who those green hills does roam,
With health and with freedom possess'd;
As for me, all I ask, all I want is my home—
O, give me my home in the West!

To pluck the wild flowers that grew in the bog,
With light heart I bounded along,
While the creak of the cricket, the croak of the frog,
Would lull me when evening was long.
Why need I recall the gone days that are past,
In this bosom lie hallowed and blest;
If I had but one wish, and that wish was my last—
O, give me my home in the West!

HOW LONG COULD I SIT ON THY BEACH, LOVELY ERIE?*

How long could I sit on thy beach, lovely Erie?
And o'er thy blue waters enrapturing gaze;
The sight is enchanting to one who is weary,
To gaze on thy flood and thy dancing blue waves.

---

*It was a lovely evening in the Autumn of 1858, when, sitting on the beach of this romantic lake, I penned the above lines.

In the distance the ships, with their full swelling sails,
  Appear like the swan with her out-spreading wings:
For, so soft over thy lake blows the favoring gales,
  And safe to her port the expected ship brings.

How fair is the sight at the close of the evening,
  Beneath the deep shade of some tall-spreading tree,
The beauties of nature to drive away grieving,
  And Erie's fair charms to illumine the e'e;
For the sun when he's setting his last golden rays
  On thy flashing waters, O, Erie! so bright,*
He seems to light up all thy waves in one blaze,
  As, kissing thy bosom, he sinks for the night.

THE NEW ENGLANDER'S FAREWELL.†

Farewell! Farewell, New England's shore!
  Farewell, land of the free!
Now I must ride the bounding wave
  And leave thee in the lea.
When I am far and far away,
  Upon the Frenchman's shore,
In dreams I'll ride the western wave
  And walk New England more.

And when, by Versailles'‡ founts I rove,
  And by Napoleon's grave,
My heart shall heave one sigh for thee
  Behind the foaming wave;

---

*A beautiful scenery, and worthy of observation.
†Composed in Belpre, Washington County, Ohio, January, 1857.
‡A place in France noted for its beautiful fountains.

And when Brittania's coast shall rear
　Its frowning points to me,
Again I'll think of the sweet land—
　My home beyond the sea.

Farewell, farewell, my lovely land,
　A long farewell to thee;
The sea that madly rolls between,
　Shall foam 'twixt thee and me.
New England, dear! New England, fair!
　'Tis for thy shores I'll die;
I cannot think of thee but what
　My heart shall rend and sigh.

WHEN I WAS A YOUNG LAD.*

Tune—*"Kinloch of Kinloch."*

When I was a young lad, with what rapture I scrambled
　The towering, the bold hills of the State of New York,
How often delighted, I'd pause as I rambled,
　To list to the song of the robin and lark;
And sweet were their notes, through each valley resounding,
　As high I ascended, 'till full in my view
I gazed at Ontario's waters rebounding,
　Afar in the distance her waves rolling blue.

What pleasure was mine, while my eyes were regaling
　Themselves, 'neath the shade of the wide-spreading trees,
At ships that afar, under white canvas sailing,
　As, spurning the waves, they bore down with the breeze;

*Written to commemorate the early scenes of my childhood.

But now I'm removed from the haunts of my childhood—
No more shall I roam the green valleys along—
No more shall I stray through the dark, pathless wildwood,
And hark to the robins' mellifluous song.

No more shall I climb the steep hills I ascended,
Where once I beheld the most beautiful scene—
The wide-spreading landscape, the prospect oft blended
With tall growing oak trees and meadows in green.
Farewell! now dear scenes, I must mourn your departure;
Ye past early visions, I'll see you no more;
But, if I should see you, 'tis not with the rapture
Once courted when young by Ontario's shore.

MY HEART I LEAVE BEHIND ME.

Tune—"*The Girl I left Behind Me.*"

Now, I must go, far, far away,
Upon the angry wide sea;
But, be it wheresoe'er I stray,
My heart I leave behind me.

But, Oh! it gives me aching pain
To leave those I love kindly,
For, Oh! I cannot love again—
My heart I leave behind me.

But that I might have still possess'd,
If I'd not loved so blindly;
But now the time is gone and past—
My heart I leave behind me.

There's Sarah, she has won my heart,
  And won it so divinely,
With all I own I now must part—
  My heart I leave behind me.

Where'er I roam, as is my lot,
  Misfortune's sure to find me ;
As Cupid drives his matchless shot,
  My heart I leave behind me.

Now I must go, far, far away,
  Upon the angry wide sea ;
But be it whereso'er I stray,
  My heart I leave behind me.

THE HEART.

In some the heart is like the flower,
  So tender and so frail ;
It blooms in sweet affection's bower,
  Or withers in a gale.
In some the heart is always gay—
  Free from the cares of life ;
With them life's one bright, sunny day,
  Devoid of sorrow, strife.

There's some who yet possess a heart,
  As hard as flint or stone—
In deeds of kindness take no part,
  Nor heed the orphan's moan.
Such hearts as this are not humane—
  The brute possesses more ;
The dog has howled o'er master slain,
  And whined at human gore.

ALONG CAYUGA'S SHORE I STRAYED.

Along Cayuga's* shore I strayed,
   With Mary on my arm reclining;
The golden sun his beams delayed,
   The sultry day seemed slow declining.
Beneath a willow tree I lay
   To watch the sparkling waves receding,
Around all nature seemed so gay,
   The golden wheat was gently waving.

And turning to my darling love,
   Sweet maid, I said, when love's first waking,
Have pity, for I swear, by Jove,
   For thee my heart is almost breaking.
Here by this lovely lake alone—
   Here on its charming shore together,
Come let us vow we will be one,
   That nought but death can us dissever.

LOVELY BOSTON BAY.

Let not the angry waves that roll
   Upon the pebbly beach,
Let not the sea-gull's restless wing,
   Nor sea-fowl's dismal screech,
Disturb thy slumbers, Annie,
   But peaceful mayst thou lay,
Beside the blue and sparkling waves,
   Of lovely Boston Bay.

-----

*This is one of that numerous group of lakes situated in central New York, in which that portion of the State so much abound. They are much celebrated for their sublime grandeur and romantic scenery.

Green ever grow the trees around,
  Throughout the rolling year,
And gently fall the morning dews,
  With soft, refreshing tear;
Upon thy grave those blooming flowers,
  O, may they ne'er decay,
With those which skirt the restless waves
  Of lovely Boston Bay.

Blow mild, each gentle zephyr,
  Blow soft, each morning gale,
That wafts the thrush's music
  From out each verdant dale;
Be still, ye boisterous whirlwinds,
  Nor mar her slumbering clay,
Which rests beside the rolling waves
  Of lovely Boston Bay.

Then let her ashes peacefully,
  In silent stillness rest,
Nor call her spirit back again,
  From the regions of the blest.
And all ye feathery songsters,
  And ye of plumage gay,
Tune low and sweet your requiem songs
  By lovely Boston Bay.

SWEET PHEBE.

Sweet Phebe, alas! you have driven
  In me love's unmerciful dart;
When I gaze on thee, angel of Heaven,
  It pierces me clean to the heart.

Why not, by this beautiful river,
    But promise me once to be mine?
In this world nothing can us dissever—
    Our vows we will hold as divine.

Then answer me, Phebe, then answer;
    Why linger the words in thy breast?
O, give me a cure for the cancer
    That's eating a hole in my chest.
If you say you're not mine, then's extended
    The disease that is tearing my heart;
But if you say yes, then 'tis ended—
    The pain will then cease for to smart.

Why, why do you keep me in waiting?
    O, answer me, Phebe, then why?
For hours I've been pleading and stating,
    Without thee I surely must die.
But if you'll not hear me, then hearken:
    To say a word more I am bent—
The rule is that always in sparking,
    Mute silence stands good for consent.

O, COME, MY LOVE, AND ROVE WITH ME.

Tune—"*Ossian's Serenade.*"

Come brave the noisy haunts of men,
And let us rove the silent glen;
Let us partake the mountain air,
And view below the valleys fair,
And view the lambs in pasture free;
O, come, my love, and rove with me.

We'll cull the wild flowers by the creek,
The vagrant zephyrs we will seek ;
Beneath the cooling shade we'll rest,
Till Phœbus' beams will seek the west ;
The fields arrayed in green we'll see—
O, come, my love, and rove with me.

Far o'er the mountain tops we'll stray,
Till dusky evening closes day ;
O, there we'll pass the fleeing hour,
While gay plumed birds in every bower,
Shall chaunt their sweetest songs to thee—
O, come, my love, and rove with me.

The mountain streams so glassy clear,
Shall murmur music in thy ear,
As o'er the craggy rocks they gleam,
And fall to join some other stream ;
Then to its mossy source we'll flee—
O, come, my love, and rove with me.

YE FACTIONS THAT TRY TO DISSOLVE THIS GREAT UNION.*

Ye factions that try to dissolve this great Union,
    May the blood of your fathers on your heads only lie ;
When the North and the South have divided communion,
    May their ghosts haunt your forms till the day that ye die.

For they gave you a gift which was well worth your keeping,
    Which you vowed to protect, which you swore to defend,
And cursed is the one who would mar them while sleeping ;
    Unwept, unlamented his life may he end.

*Written during the political agitation of 1860.

If but once those warm ties which connect us are broken,
  Where's the one who'll select the wide breach to repair?
When the fire of resentment and hatred's awaken,
  Unextinguished, for ages 'twill eternally glare.

O, then, never, ye sons of Columbia, O, never!
  Be ye found to perform such a vile, cursed deed,
Of this great, glorious Union the links to dissever,
  To join which our fathers did perish and bleed.

LIBERTY'S SHRINE.

From Texas, that throws out her wide spreading prairie,
  To Maine, which exults in her forests of pine,
Exists there a race. 'Tis the home of the freeman,
  'Tis the land which lies sacred to Liberty's shrine.

And long as our Eagle shall over us hover,
  The star of our Empire shall never descend;
While bright are our streams, or green are our valleys,
  To none but our God will our knee ever bend.

Then woe to the despot who'd try to enslave us,
  And woe to the tyrant that would us enthrall;
For thousands of swords would leap forth from their scabbards,
  And thousands of freemen rise at freedom's first call.

The mountains would teem with the millions descending,
  The earth would be darkened with freemen in arms,
And over our hills, fields and prairies, far wending,
  They'd rise in their might, roused by war's stern alarms.
  2

FLOAT ON, NOBLE BANNER.

To the American Flag.

Float on, noble banner, protected by millions—
  Display thy proud folds to the wind;
Not the foul, crouching traitor—the basest of villains—
  Can tear thee from where thou art pinned.

For sacred thou art, O, thou banner long cherished
  With fond and unquenchable pride;
It was 'neath thy stripes where our forefathers perished,
  And 'neath thy bright stars where they died.

Then how could we stand by, beholding thee riven,
  Thou flag so immortally blest?
No, never! while blazes the sun in yon Heaven,
  Or blood courses through any breast.

And when the war sounds through Columbia, alarming
  Her sons to the battle to fly,
While gazing upon thee for battle he's arming,
  He'll turn from thy folds for to sigh.

For a moment he'll think of his fathers departed—
  Of blood that was spilt in his cause;
But short is the while he will stand stricken-hearted—
  That moment is sorrow's sad pause.

From his eyes he will dry the sad tears that were gushing—
  In vengeance they'll flash for the slain;
And shouting his watch-cry to battle when rushing—
  My fathers, you've died not in vain!

O, WELL MAY YE BOAST, YE PROUD SONS OF CO-LUMBIA.*

O, well may ye boast, ye proud sons of Columbia,
   Let England's old Lion in her fierceness delight,
But ye are as free as the eagle—your emblem—
   That soars to the sun in her far, lofty flight.

But O, then remember, ye sons of brave freemen,
   How costly and dearly that freedom was bought;
Just think on the red fields of White Plains and Camden,
   And Bunker Hill bloody, where bravely they fought.

But now they have gone—those dear martyrs have perished,
   And Washington, dearest of all—he has fled;
Then let us remember our rights and our country—
   Embalm in our bosoms the names of those dead.

The bold, bold American, proud of his country,
   Laughs at the slaves as they kneel to their lords;
He scorns the foul treason oppression doth gather,
   And turns with disgust from the gold which it hoards.

WHEN DARK CLOUDS OF SORROW.

When dark clouds of sorrow and trouble roll o'er us—
Misfortunes unnumbered should gather before us—
'Tis pleasant to think that a true friend is left us—
That adversity's hand's not entirely bereft us.

---

*This was one of my earliest compositions, and the first that appeared in print; being published in a Virginia newspaper, bordering the Ohio River.

HOW SECURE DOES COLUMBIA SLUMBER.

How secure does Columbia slumber,
  Nor fear any danger that's nigh,
While true hearts there are without number,
  To defend her, her freedom, or die.

O, then ye who would threaten commotion,
  And disunion exultantly greet,
She stands firm as a rock in the ocean,
  On which billows unceasingly beat.

By the millions her true sons would rally,
  If strife should endanger her shore;
They would pour from each mountain and valley,
  And fight like their fathers of yore.

Columbia, thy Union's forever!
  And blest are the true and the brave;
And cursed is the one who'd dissever,
  The gift which our forefathers gave.

THE KISS.

Allow me to imprint a kiss
Upon thy rosy cheek, dear Miss;
Then to express the joy I'd feel—
The wounds of sorrow it would heal.
I'm sure 'twould give me great relief,
And banish future cause of grief;
But, oh! the woe if you'd refuse!
The former wounds it would unloose;
They'd freshly bleed, and daily gain—
Still keep increasing with the pain.

BESIDE THE SUSQUEHANNA.

The flowers are blooming fresh and fair,
The lambs are sporting everywhere—
Come, let us hie away from care,
  Beside the Susquehanna.

While April, joyous in her birth,
Awakes each tender stem from earth,
And rampant all appears with mirth,
  Beside the Susquehanna.

Then come with me, my own true love,
And stray with me each shady grove;
Far o'er the mounds and banks we'll rove,
  Which skirt the Susquehanna.

The robin there shall tune his song—
The echoing vales the notes prolong—
While to the sound shall dance along,
  The sparkling Susquehanna.

'Tis there where lovers love to meet ;
'Tis there where lovers choose to greet,
And spend the passing hours so sweet,
  Beside the Susquehanna.

Then hie with me, my dark-eyed maid ;
We'll seek the cool and welcome shade,
Where we can rove the fragrant glade,
  Beside the Susquehanna.

Naught can disturb our calm repose,
Where blooms the lonely woodland rose ;
Then come, till evening's curtains close
  Along the Susquehanna.

ERIE'S SHORE.

O, how I love
At eve to rove,
Where Erie rolls her water!
Give me no more
Than Erie's shore,
To roam with Idon's daughter.

When night unbars
Her golden stars,
Across her waters darkling,
On Erie bright,
At ope of night,
A thousand gems lie sparkling.

O, lovely lake,
How gently break,
The waves against thy border!
Upon the rock
They softly knock,
Though storms may make them louder.

And when I mark
The fisher's bark,
Across the blue waves dashing,
As to the shore
He bends his oar,
The spray around him flashing.

O, how I love
At eve to rove,
Where Erie rolls her water!
Give me no more
Than Erie's shore,
To roam with Idon's daughter.

BANKS OF MOHAWK.*

Tune—"Kinloch of Kinloch."

When merry and gay in the days of my childhood,
  How oft, in the cool of the evening, I'd walk
To cull the wild flowers which grew in the wildwood,
  Or carelessly strayed by the banks of Mohawk.

How mellow the chime of the village bells ringing,
  The lark's evening song, with the woodpecker's knock
On the old hollow tree, while the country maid's singing
  Mellifluous 'rose from the banks of Mohawk.

And many an hour of the noon-day I've squandered,
  As, poised in the shade, I would gaze at my flock,
Or, oft on the beach, as I daily have wandered,
  The pebbles to find by the banks of Mohawk.

But what were those scenes, when compared with the pleasure
  I fancied I felt as I'd merrily talk
With my wild rustic bride, or would wander at leisure
  Down by the green lawn on the banks of Mohawk.

But gone are those days which I once fondly cherished—
  As Time flies, he seems but my feelings to mock,
For never again will those days that have perished,
  Return with the years to the banks of Mohawk.

———

DEAR PERSIS, I'VE PRAYED AND PETITIONED.

Dear Persis, I've prayed and petitioned,
  But nothing from thee could I gain ;
The more I have begged and have pleaded,
  The more I have pleaded in vain.

———

*While on a visit to Piqua, Miami county, Ohio, September, 1860, I
penned the above lines.

Then grant me, O loveliest Persis,
 The pitiful boon that I crave?
If not, then I swear, soon or later,
 'Twill keep dragging me down to the grave.

I know you're unconscious, dear Persis,
 The love that I bear unto thee;
You feel not the fire that is burning—
 That's burning, consuming in me.
And wilt thou then know but the physie,
 The only good remedy sure—
Know then, Oh! my life and my darling,
 In you lies the power and the cure.

It's useless to argue any longer,
 I've waited so long upon you,
Till patience no longer's a virtue—
 What more could you want me to do?
This life's but a long rolling river—
 A ceaseless, meandering stream,
And if you'll accompany me down it,
 You can live like a Princess or Queen.

WHERE SCHUYLKILL MEETS THE DELAWARE.*

In vain I roam in every land,
From shore to shore, from strand to strand,
In vain I cross the foaming brine
To search each realm, survey each clime;

*During my tour through the Eastern States, in 1858, I stopped at Philadelphia. Standing in close proximity to where the above-named rivers I meet, I composed the following stanzas.

My tottering steps would fain retrace
The weary miles back to that place,
Back to that place—none can compare—
Where Schuylkill meets the Delaware.

Delightful spot! can I forget
The bliss, the joy that there I've met,
When early love begins to shoot,
Within the heart it takes its root,
So deeply set naught can it grub,
Though years and time against it rub.
So for that spot my heart does tear,
Where Schuylkill meets the Delaware.

Oh! there, with Mary by my side,
I rambled by the rising tide;
Now she is gone and I am here,
Far from the spot I love so dear.
I love the scenes, for round my heart
Entwined they never can depart,
And thou my love, sleep on my fair,
Where Schuylkill meets the Delaware.

A LOCK OF THY HAIR, TO REMEMBER THEE BY.

A lock of thy hair, to remember thee by;
    Yes, darling, I cannot forget,
When far among strangers, I'll think, with a sigh,
    Of affectionate friends which I've met.

And, though I may carry this token with me,
    Or commit it away to the flame,
All the same I'll still cherish the mem'ry of thee,
    And hold in affection thy name.

NEW JERSEY, THY BORDERS ARE WILD AND RO-
MANTIC.

Away, ye gay landscapes, ye gardens of roses,
In you let the minions of luxury rove ;
Restore me the rocks where the snow-flake reposes,
Though still they are sacred to freedom and love.

BYRON.

New Jersey, thy borders are wild and romantic—
   With what high excitement I've mounted each hill—
The roar of the Ocean, the mighty Atlantic,
   With scenes so exciting the breast cannot fill.
Full oft have I climbed o'er your northern mountains,
   With gun on my shoulder and dog by my side ;
And oft, when athirst, I would drink from the fountains
   Which oozed from the base of the lofty hill's side.

And then when the heat of the noon-day was falling,
   Compelled, I would seek for the shade of a tree,
'Till, borne on the breeze, the loud vesper bells ringing,
   Again to the hunt I would hasten in glee.
'Twas then over hill, over rock, bush and thistle,
   Till night threw her mantle of shadow o'er the rills,
I'd dash on my way 'til I heard the loud whistle
   Of the shepherd boy calling his dog o'er the hills.

Then down from the mountains I'd swoop like the vulture,
   With Carlo I'd race for the cabin hard by ;
I envied no lord with his learning and culture,
   Nor luxurious tables inviting him nigh.
For peace and contentment—those sweet boons of pleasure—
   I had in abundance on this side the grave,
And the pure bubbling water was mine without measure—
   What more could I ask, or what more could I crave ?

THE ORPHAN'S LAMENT.

A lost one, I sat on the grave of my mother,
  I sobbed and I sighed as I sat there alone;
The favors of fortune one tear could not smother,
  For I felt, as I sat there, no place to call home.

Alas! I exclaimed, in the depth of my sorrow,
  The beasts of the field have a place of their own;
The bird has a nest and the rabbit a burrow,
  But I have no place I can call as a home.

But long since thou left me, my own dearest mother,
  For far from thy grave my last footsteps did roam;
Again and again I might wander it over,
  But never I'll find but one place to call home.

Ah! here on thy grave as I sit broken-hearted,
  With no one to cheer me nor with me to moan;
My sisters and brothers by long miles are parted,
  And I have no place I can call as my home.

But Ill not regret it, thou friend of my childhood,
  I will not regret thou hast left me forlorn,
This life's but a dreary and desolate wildwood,
  And why should I mourn on this earth for a home.

Then sleep on, sweet mother, for time will keep rolling,
  And soon 'twill roll o'er me and mark me as one;
But when the grave calls me the thought is consoling,
  To find with my mother in heaven a sweet home.

MY LOVE TO YOU I CAN'T EXPRESS.

My love to you I can't express,
   For often does my bosom swell
And feels for who? Ah! feels for thee,
   But few there are its love can tell.

How often do I sit alone
   When birds have ceased their songs so gay,
And evening's shade has spread around,
   To think of thee so far away.

Though solitary as I sit,
   Methinks thy image oft I see,
O, for one moment with thee love,
   Since I can love none now but thee.

But thee, ah! well I might say thee,
   For who beside thee can I love;
My heart is thine, my vows are made
   And witnessed by that power above.

I've loved thee since I set my eyes
   Upon that goddess form of thine,
And never for a moment thought
   You'd be another's love, but mine.

I cannot let such thoughts obtain
   For once an entrance in my mind;
I'm pledged to thee and thou to me
   By all the ties affection bind.

VALE OF MONROE.*

O, dear, lovely vale! how I swell with emotion,
　　When I think of thy streams, where I oft loved to go!
How the sun would arise, with his beams in commotion—
　　In splendor would dance in the vale of Monroe!

But now I am far from thee—still thou art alluring,
　　And I sigh for the roses that bright there did grow;
But oft, as I call you to mem'ry, I'm viewing
　　Thy glories and beauties, dear vale of Monroe!

Wherever I roam, I can never forget thee—
　　I can never forget thee in this world below;
Though other climes spread out their gay scenes around me,
　　I'll remember thee ever, sweet vale of Monroe!

Farewell, lovely valley! in memory still living,
　　I may roam far away where no one doth know;
But wherever I roam, my heart will keep giving
　　A long glance and sigh for the vale of Monroe!

MY DARLING, INDEED IT IS CERTAIN.

My darling, indeed it is certain,
　　For sure the truth I would tell—
A viper has got in my bosom,
　　And made it far worse than a hell.
For I swear, since I first got acquainted,
　　Or gazed on thy beautiful face,
My poor bleeding heart it has fastened,
　　And held in its dreadful embrace.

*Written in memory of Monroe county, N. Y., where I spent my early days; composed while residing by the Ohio River.

And thou art the one who has stolen,
  And robbed me of peace and of rest;
Ever since I have gazed on thy features,
  The serpent's abode in my breast.
And I vow, till it does get unfastened,
  No pleasure for me can remain;
Ev'ry time that I try to dislodge it,
  It gives me additional pain.

'Tis vain to attempt now a rescue—
  I'm certain my last hour is come;
But short is the time I must tarry,
  And thou art the cause, cruel one.
Why gaze on me, love, so cold-hearted?
  'Tis you know the remedy sure;
Why gaze on my misery smiling?
  Alas! I must die without cure.

A LONE WANDERER, I SAT ON THE BANKS OF OHIO.

A lone wand'rer, I sat on the banks of Ohio;
  The sun was fast sinking his rays in the west;
I gazed on the swift, gliding flight of the swallow,
  As gently and smoothly it skimmed o'er her breast.

And there, as I sat by that "beautiful river,"
  How much, I exclaimed, from thee I can learn!
Thy streams emblematic of day that shall never—
  Yes; weeks, months, and years, that shall never return.

While thus lonely musing, my memory wandering
  To scenes of my youth, and my past boyhood days,
And lost in deep thought, o'er my infancy pondering,
  Upon the clear waters beneath me I gazed.

But while thus reflecting, I thought of my Nancy;
   I thought of my Nancy by Erie's fair shore;
The cot and the garden arose in my fancy—
   I thought I beheld my dear love for once more.

O, hard, cruel fortune! why art thou so trifling
   With the feelings of one who is doomed to despair?
The dreadful reality often keeps stifling
   In my bosom the soft, soothing dreams that wake there.

O, had I the wings of a dove or an eagle,
   How soon I would spread them, nor even delay,
Till I would alight 'fore a door that's congenial,
   To soothe the sad cares of a wand'rer away.

———

THE LAPLANDER LOVES HIS COLD, ICY RETREAT.

The Laplander loves his cold, icy retreat,
   The Esquimaux his chilly plain;
Then why should I not love each valley so sweet—
   Each snow-covered mountain of Maine?

I ask not the pleasures which dwell in the South,
   That poets have fabled of yore;
Away with their flowers, which my heart sick'ning loaths,
   But give me my cold home before.

No pleasure for me have their hot, burning skies,
   Nor flowers that in blooming will last;
Their warm, sultry breezes my soul does despise,
   And mourns for old Winter's cold blast.

It sighs for the mountains that towering rise,
  Above the wide plain or the valleys of snow,
And nothing in life does the soul dearer prize,
  Than infancy's haunts, where it once loved to go.

And though we may climb to the temple of fame,
  And wear honor's wreath on our brow,
We'll bear in affection the dear cottage name,
  Where we plighted our first solemn vow.

FLOW ON, LOVELY HUDSON!*

TUNE—"*Sweet Vale of Avoca.*"

Flow on, lovely Hudson—thou lovely stream, flow!
Encompassed by banks that look verdant below;
Let poets of Thames and of Seine† sing their lay,
But I know thou'rt arrayed far fairer than they.

Then flow in thy beauty, sweet river—flow on!
Whom Nature her charms has so lavished upon;
And they who beside thee might happen to stray,
Bewitched by thy beauties, unwilling must stay.

O, had I a home by thy border so fair,
In pleasure and peace I'd contented dwell there;
How calm flow thy waters, O, river so bright!
Thy enameled green banks are the stranger's delight.

---

*While on a pleasure trip down the Hudson, in 1858, I composed the above lines.
†The well known rivers of England and France.

How majestic the mountains that border thy waves!
The towering Highlands,* whose dark summit braves
The mad, angry tempest—the wild whirlwind's shock;
Those dark, lofty battlements their wrath only mock.

To leave thy clear waters it saddens my heart,
Where Phœbus himself lingering, is loth to depart;
But time tarries not—I must bid you adieu—
Farewell, Hudson, then, and thy waves rolling blue!

AND WILL YOU ROVE WITH ME, SWEET MAID?

Tune—"*Highland Mary.*"

And will you rove with me, sweet maid,
　　Down by yon silvery water?
And there beneath the beechen shade,
　　Till gathering night we'll loiter;
Till night will spread her mantled pall,
　　Along the shore we'll tarry,
And if you'll vow to be my all,
　　I'll be your constant Harry.

I'll be your own, come weal or woe,
　　If you'll be mine forever;
And let what will may come or go,
　　We'll pledge our vows together.
Then will you rove with me, sweet maid,
　　Down by yon silvery water?
And there beneath the beechen shade,
　　Till gathering night we'll loiter.

---

*These mountains are much noted for their picturesque scenery, and wild grandeur.

HOIST THAT PROUD FLAG.

Hoist that proud flag, 'tis the flag of the free;
Hoist that proud flag, 'tis the banner for me.
Awake, all ye sons of Columbia; arise,
Hoist that proud flag—let it float in the skies.

Behold it, as proudly it floats in the air;
O who dare attempt for to draw it from there?
Or where is the one who so vile as would durst
Tear down that proud banner to tramp in the dust?

Was't not 'neath its folds where each victory was won,
Achieved by that hero, our own Washington?
Let it wave so when minions shall threaten alarm;
Hoist, hoist that proud flag, it will shield it from harm.

Around it will rally the true and the brave,
Beneath it to conquer or find there a grave;
Our right arm is pledged to protect its bright folds
On the land, or the sea, where the wide ocean rolls.

O FAR, FAR AWAY, BY POTOMAC'S CALM BREAST.

Tune—"*To the West.*"

O far, far away, by Potomac's calm breast,
By its smooth-gliding waters my Fanny finds rest;
Dire troubles and dangers no more her assail,
Undisturbed she reclines in that calm, peaceful vale.

How fair is the spot where she silently sleeps,
Where willows around her unceasingly weep;
There, winding unseen, the Potomac extends
Her clear, glancing waters where the swamp willow blends.

You may roam through this world—you may roam every-
    where—
But no place can you find that's more charmingly fair;
There spring's clothed in verdure, the flowers ne'er decay—
When this sad life is vanished, O there let me lay.

O there let me lay, where its clear waters lave
The green flowery banks, where tall lindens wave;
Where the jessamine nods to the murmuring breeze,
As it whispers her requiem through the green leaves.

THAT IS THE FLAG.

TUNE—"*Shed not a Tear.*"

Is yon waving banner the flag that we own?
    That is the flag, that is the flag,
Which through the red field was victoriously borne?
    That is the flag, that is the flag.

Was't not 'neath its folds where our forefathers died—
Where death was to them but the highest of pride—
Where, smiling, they nobly expired by its side?
    That is the flag, that is the flag.

Has it not waved out upon every breeze?
    That is the flag, that is the flag;
And floated in triumph all over the seas?
    That is the flag, that is the flag.

Is it not the hope of the bond and the slave—
The ensign that headed the gallant and brave
While wading through blood, that their country might save?
    That is the flag, that is the flag.

Has it not flashed out over Bunker's red hill?
That is the flag, that is the flag;
Where first our country's blood did spill?
That is the flag, that is the flag.

Then will't not in beauty and glory still fly,
Unmolested and free in our own sunny sky,
Above those brave martyrs who for it did die?
That is the flag, that is the flag.

SING LOW, SWEET BIRD, BESIDE THAT STREAM.

Sing low, sweet bird, beside that stream,
For on its banks doth Nancy dream;
Beneath yon willow tree that weeps
And droops in sorrow, Nancy sleeps.

Ye flowers and roses, bloom more fair,
Your queen and fairest gem lies there;
Spread wide your leaves, and bathe her tomb
With fragrant spices and perfume.

Assume thy beauty, lily fair,
And bow thy head in sorrow there;
For neath that grassy turf lies low
The fairest flower that e'er did grow.

And thou bright, warbling streams that flows,
Take heed, for on thy banks repose
A tender flower I once possessed—
I'd have you not disturb her rest.

But you, mild, gentle evening breeze,
I still would have you through the trees
To sigh her requiem, till the close
Of dewy ev'ning folds the rose.

Sing low, sweet bird, beside that stream,
For on its banks does Nancy dream;
Beneath yon willow tree that weeps
And droops in sorrow, Nancy sleeps.

FAREWELL, DEAR ANGELINE, FAREWELL.

TUNE—"*Come, take a Sail.*"

Farewell, dear Angeline, farewell;
    Perhaps no more I'll see
Thy diamond eyes, thy pearl-like neck,
    Thy form, that's dear to me.
But yet good fortune may be kind,
    And bring me back again,
Once more to gaze upon thy face,
    Thy arms once more regain.

Then let me kiss thee for the last,
    The time is drawing nigh;
And let me take the last embrace
    Before from thee I fly.
I soon will be in distant climes—
    O how it rends my heart—
And, though I seldom wept before,
    The tears begin to start.

But, though I leave you, oft I'll view
    Thy features in my dreams;
And, turning oft, I'll think of thee,
    And of those parting scenes.
Farewell then, Angeline, farewell;
    Perhaps again I'll see
Thy diamond eyes, thy pearl-like neck,
    Thy form that's dear to me.

MY MARY'S GONE   MY MARY'S GONE!

Tune—"*Shells of Ocean.*"

My Mary's gone! my Mary's gone!
  She sleeps beneath the linden tree ;
No more I hear her lute-like tones
  At ev'ning's hour to welcome me.
Forever's hushed that mellow voice,
  That voice I never more shall hear ;
No more, returning home from toil,
  'Twill greet me with its welcome cheer.

Sad is my soul since we did part—
  Grim Death, thou hast no terror now ;
I ask not life, then cut me down ;
  I'm but a barren, withering bough.
The rose that strewed my path of life,
  And soothed me on the bed of pain,
At last has vanished from my view,
  And nothing but the thorns remain.

O Mary, dear! O Mary, dear!
  I never more shall see again ;
Does she but know what I endure—
  The racks of agony and pain ?
But no ; she feels not what I feel,
  Nor felt the thorn that pierced my side
When, leaning on my trembling arms,
  She lowly bade farewell—and died.

But why mourn her, then, 'cause, forsooth,
  She's safely crossed this " vale of tears,"
And, in that brighter land above,
  Dwells free from further cares and fears.

Then I'll no longer mourn for her,
But, oh, life has a burden grown ;
I cannot stay—I will not stay—
To linger out this life alone.

BATTLE SONG.

FOR THE UNION VOLUNTEERS.

O, we're the brave boys who are used to alarms,
When our country's in danger we'll stand to our arms,
For traitors and rebels can never defile
Our star-spangled banner, our blood-purchased soil.

CHORUS—Then hurrah! then hurrah! to the battle we'll go,
We either must perish or conquer the foe.

The New Englanders pour from their wild, craggy rocks,
With their trustworthy barrels and rusty old locks ;
They are the brave gallants who never did yield
To a foe or a tyrant, on any red field.

CHORUS—Then hurrah! &c.

Pennsylvania she rallies her sons for the fight—
By the thousands they come from the left and the right,
While New York gathers out, from each hamlet and glen,
Her dashing young lads and her well chosen men.

CHORUS—Then hurrah! &c.

Indiana pours forth her brave sons at the call,
To fight for our country or for her to fall ;
Kentucky, the land and the birth-place of Clay,
Is gathering the flower of her youth for the fray.

CHORUS—Then hurrah! &c.

Illinois' ready sons are forsaking awhile
Their wide-spreading prairies and bountiful soil,
While Michigan, restless the Union to save,
Is gathering by thousands her gallant and brave.
CHORUS—Then hurrah! &c.

Young Wisconsin and Iowa hears the war sound,
With young Minnesota on the red battle ground;
They muster their thousands, to shelter from harm
Our Union and banner, with old Uncle Sam.
CHORUS—Then hurrah! &c.

The brave Buckeye lads all so willing they come,
With bayonets bright gleaming, and swords buckled on;
From the North, East and West see the multitudes crowd,
With the stars and the stripes o'er their heads waving proud.
CHORUS—Then hurrah! &c.

THE AMERICAN'S FAREWELL TO HIS NATIVE COUNTRY ON GOING TO VISIT EUROPE.

Farewell, land of Washington, Webster and Clay;
Farewell, land of freedom, I cannot delay;
I must meet the wide ocean whose billows I fear
Will bear me away from the land I love dear.

Adieu! then Ohio, whose calm waters bright
To some more mighty stream take their far winding flight;
And thou, placid Hudson, I soon will despair
For thy green charming banks so lovely and fair.

No more shall I roam where my forefather's strayed,
And gaze on the scenes where I oft have delayed;
My bark dances on, and I hear the loud roar
Of the breakers that dash on my own native shore.

Then again is the sad tear quick forced from my eyes,
As my bark o'er the waves like a swift arrow flies,
While the last sinking glimpse of my fair shores I catch,
All the dear parting scenes to remembrance now fetch.

CAN I FORGET THE LAND WHERE I?

Can I forget the land where I
   Was reared, amid the lofty hills,
And made the wily deer to fly,
   Which sought the cool and gurgling rills?
Can I, in France's sunny vales,
   Or on the balmy mounts of Spain,
Forget Ohio's balmy gales,
   That often fanned my burning brain?

O, no; though I should ever stray,
   And never find a place of rest,
I'll ne'er forget, though far away,
   The scenes with which I once was blest.
When wandering o'er my native hills,
   Or sitting in the cooling shade,
Or musing by the babbling rills,
   Meand'ring through my native glade.

Not that I dream of finding e'er
   Another place to dote upon,
For such fair scenes, I well may fear,
   Upon has never shone the sun.
Perhaps these tame domestic charms
   Possess the heart of some born child;
But O, give me Ohio's farms,
   Its rip'ning grain, her forests wild.

3

LAND OF LIBERTY.

Prepare the ship,
The waves we'll rip,
To the land of Liberty;
And onward bound,
Till my home is found,
In the land of Liberty.

On! on to my home;
The waves yet foam,
To the land of Liberty.
O, yet move on,
Ever and anon,
To the land of Liberty.

O, take me there,
Where damsels fair,
Roam the land of Liberty.
There place my grave,
Where lives the brave,
In the land of Liberty.

And when I meet
My land so sweet,
O, the land of Liberty;
And if I'll part,
'Twill break my heart,
From the land of Liberty.

CALIFORNIA'S SHORE.

Away, away, my gallant bark,
Fear not the angry weather;
Spread all thy sail to catch the wind,
The clouds begin to gather.

Afar astern the breakers dash—
I hear their distant roar;
Then speed thee on, my gallant bark,
To California's shore.

Then on, sail on, my noble craft,
There's none can sail more prouder;
I know thou'st braved the winds before,
When storms were thrice more louder.
Then flinch not now to meet the gale
Which thou hast met before,
But bear me on, through storm or shine,
To California ' shore.

Still louder does the storm-fiend shriek,
Still higher waves are bounding,
As from the starboard side I hear
The dashing waves resounding.
Then welcome to old Ocean's shock,
We'll fear her wrath no more,
But bravely ride, through thick and thin,
To California's shore.

————

O, EMMA, THY BROW IS LIKE MARBLE.

O, Emma, thy brow is like marble,
Thy cheeks like the lily so pale;
The birds of the forest that warble,
And sing in thy own native vale,
Their voice it is not near so charming,
Nor half of the power to console,
But thine's like a fire that is warming,
And cheering the sorrowing soul.

When grief seems to haunt and to chase me,
  And on me does heavily lay,
When charms of thy voice does possess me,
  It drives the foul demon away.
O, had I the fortune to own thee,
  Or say that my all it is thine,
There's nothing could make me disown thee,
  More dear than Potosi's rich mine.

For whole loads of Mexican treasure
  I'd give, or tramp under my feet,
If I had but that moment of pleasure
  Of printing a kiss on thy cheek.
In vain I might search this world over,
  For virtue more purer than thine—
That, I'm sure, I could never discover;
  O, if I could call thee but mine.

THE EMIGRANT'S FAREWELL, ON LEAVING OLD ENGLAND.

Come, now, my boys, we'll sing a song,
  As long's old England's seen,
And when she sinks behind the wave,
  Our songs shall still be green.

Our songs shall still be green, my boys,
  Our ship with waves must play,
We'll leave old England fading
  Behind the drifting spray.

Behind the drifting spray, my boys,
  Our ship must strike the foam,
We'll sail across the bounding wave,
  Far from our native home.

Come, now, my gallant boys, bear down
  Unto the land of the free—
Unto the wide, extended plains
  Of broad America.

Of broad America, my boys—
  And O, my gallant tars,
'Tis the land of Washington the wise,
  The floating stripes and stars.

THROUGH THE WAVING FIELDS OF GREEN.

Tune—*"Faintly Flow, thou Falling River."*
Have we not roved together, Sallie—
  Watched the twilight's closing scene,
On the hill and in the valley,
  Through the waving fields of green?

On the hill have we not pondered,
  By the mill and deep ravine—
Or, as chance would have it, wandered
  Through the waving fields of green?

Hours have we not sat together,
  When the evening's golden sheen
Fell upon the halcyon river,
  And on waving fields of green?

O, FROWN NOT ON ME NOW, LOVE.

O, frown not on me now, love,
  O, frown not on me now,
For gaze on death I'd rather,
  Than passion on thy brow.

What is it does displease thee?
  It cannot, love, be me;
Recall that frown—that frown, love,
  I cannot brook to see.

I've waited for thy coming,
  And longed for thy embrace,
But cannot bear to see thee
  With wrath upon thy face.
Then chase away the cloud that
  Thy features hover round,
And loose the smiles of gladness
  That in thy heart abound.

I never saw thee look so—
  What can the matter be?
Are evils dire pursuing,
  Or fortune fled from thee?
If so, to do their utmost
  Bid them, and breast the storm;
Perhaps the clouds but cover
  Hearts sympathizing warm.

Then cheer up—sink not, frown not,
  Misfortune bravely stand;
Help first yourself, and Heaven
  Will lend a helping hand.
Remember he who strives well,
  To stem life's angry tide,
For his reward must tarry,
  Or until death abide.

O, LET ME TO THE WOODLAND FLEE.

O, let me to the woodland flee,
  Far from the busy throng,
I love to see the tow'ring tree,
  And hear the robin's song;
I love to see the lambs at play,
  Or skipping o'er the green,
And watch the op'ning flower of day,
  And twilight's gorgeous scene.

I love to wander o'er the hills,
  Inhale the stainless air,
Imbibe from pure and gurgling rills,
  Meandering coolly there;
I love to watch the setting sun,
  As slowly in the west,
Whene'er his daily course is run,
  Sink to his nightly rest.

I love to gather the wild flowers
  That unbidden bloom alone,
And listen, through the evening hours,
  To the wild dove's melancholy tone;
I love to watch the lowing herds,
  While seated in the verdant lawn,
And listen to the vocal birds,
  Sing tireless through the orient morn.

YE DEPARTED, WHO PERISHED AND DIED FOR YOUR COUNTRY.

Ye departed, who perished and died for your country,
  May Columbia honor your graves with her tears;
It is not your heroic deeds that she honors,
  But the cause and the reason you died she reveres.

O, for the spirit which nerved you in battle,
  T● inspire your descendants with motives the same,
Who willingly laid down your lives for your country,
  Nor fought ye for honor, nor died ye for fame.

And gone though you be, may your mem'ry undying,
  Remain still beloved in the hearts of your sons,
Your heroic deeds be remembered forever,
  As lasting as liberty tyranny shuns.

May the fields where they fought, where their life-blood was
    given,
  Be indelibly graven on History's scroll,
Their patriot cause stand a monument lasting,
  Through the cycle of ages in future to roll.

WAR SONG.

Awake, all ye sons of proud freemen, awaken !
Americans, rise ! for the Union is shaken,
And over your heads the fair peace-clouds are breaking ;
  Come forth ! 'tis your country that calls.

Come forth ! hear you not your dead forefathers crying
From out of the bloody graves where they are lying ?
Arise ! 'neath the stars and the stripes that are flying,
  ,We'll swear that this Union remains.

Come forth ! all ye children of heroes departed,
And you, ye descendants of patriots martyred,
Behold their dear purchase by ruffians bartered-
  And sold, with their blood spilt in vain.

Come forth! cries the chieftains who led you to battle,
And stand undismayed by the cannons' loud rattle;
Strike down the foul traitors who would lightly prattle
  Of severing this Union cemented by blood.

Rise, sons of Columbia—arise in your glory!
Let your children's children circle the story,
How fathers, with pride, and their grand-fathers hoary,
  Delighted to die for their country's good.

Unsheath, then, the sword; shout your watch-cry, that never,
While true freemen live, will this Union dissever,
"But one and insep'rable, now and forever,"
  She'll stand on the records of Time.

MEET ME BY THE SILVERY TIDE.

To-night, when Luna's mounting high,
When fewer clouds obscure the sky,
When she shines forth in all her pride,
Meet me by the silvery tide.

Meet me in the silent hour,
Meet me in the lonely bower,
Meet me where the waters glide,
Meet me by the silvery tide.

When all nature sinks to rest,
When happy dreams and visions blest
Appear but shortly to abide,
Meet me by the silvery tide.

Where no ear can hear our vows,
Where no one may know our loves,
Where we can wander side by side,
Meet me by the silvery tide.

There, beside the sandy shore,
We'll whisper, love, as oft before,
Nor mark how fast the time may slide;
Meet me by the silvery tide.

Then to you I will reveal,
What yet no man did ever feel;
If so, the stars refuse to hide,
Meet me by the silvery tide.

COME, JANE, THE FLOWERS ARE BLOOMING.

TUNE—*"The Summer Days are Coming."*

Come, Jane, the flowers are blooming,
 The bespangled heath's in green,
The lawn is just assuming
 The loveliest colors seen.
The florid morn is breaking,
 The sun will soon arise,
The lark is just awak'ning,
 And hast'ning to the skies.

The thrush, perched on the bramble,
 Is pouring forth her lay,
Dear Jane, come, let us ramble,
 Conversing by the way.
I'll whisper of the pleasure
 Enjoyed in days gone by,
And strolling at our leisure,
 Thy charms I'll deify.

I'll praise thy auburn tresses,
 So graceful and divine,
Thy blue eyes, which distresses
 This love-sick heart of mine.

Then come, the flowers are blooming,
The bespangled heath's in green,
The lawn is just assuming
The loveliest colors seen.

ALONG FAIR HUDSON'S VERDANT BANKS.

Along enameled Hudson's verdant banks
I strayed, at evening's closing hour,
Fair Nature smiled in every scene,
And songsters sung in every bower.

Delighted with the gliding stream,
That rolled in silent grandeur on,
While gazing on the silv'ry tide,
I'd listen to the robin's song.

But, though the prospect smiled so fair,
Enough to cheer the saddest heart,
I'd often pause to think of one,
And oft'ner bid my grief depart.

For there is one, though only one,
That I might give this world to see—
She dwells by Mississippi's stream,
So many cruel leagues from me.

Ah, me! but could I view her face,
Her rosy cheek, her smiling eye,
While folded in her loving arms,
I there might wish myself to die.

erhaps the hour may yet arrive,
 When I may view her form once more,
And dry the wasting grief that's preyed
 So oft upon my bosom's core.

Then roll on, time, there's few can tell
 What fortune thou hast for them hid;
I doubt not but thou hast for me
 Untold of joys behind thy lid.

YE GALLANT FEW, WHO FOUGHT AND BLED.

Ye gallant few, who fought and bled
 To free your country in distress,
Long may the world, with drooping head,
 Though hung in grief, your mem'ry bless.
Long may your sons, with ardent souls,
 Inspired by your heroic deeds,
Protect the flag beneath whose folds
 The hero-freeman fights and bleeds.

Long may their breasts be willing found,
 A shield to guard their country's rights,
When danger calls to forward bound,
 Protect her from oppression's blights.
Then will their children's children bow,
 Through generations yet to be,
In meek and holy reverence low,
 In honor of the noble free.

They'll bless you for the boon you gave,—
 That sacred boon of Liberty,
Which raised them from a servile slave,
 To glory in the name of free.

They'll bless you for the lesson taught,
　To rather die than live in chains,
That to the tyrant's will there's naught
　But cursed slavery remains.

ALL OF THE FRIENDS ATTACHED TO ME.

All of the friends attached to me,
　They all have flown,
Save only one; that one is thee,
　And thee alone.
Alas! that such inconstancy
　Should be our lot;
How soon, when riches from us flee,
　We are forgot.

IF YOU LOVE ME AS I LOVE THEE.

If you love me as I love thee—
　　　　Then what?
The nuptial state would be our fate,
　　　　Our lot.

'Spose I should say thy hope's no ray
　　　　From thee?
And further own you love alone—
　　　　Ah! me.

'Spose I declare thy love I share—
　　　　Hist! hear!
My heart does burn with love in turn,
　　　　My dear!

I'm glad, my dear—rejoiced to hear—
   Thou'rt mine.
Then I'll admit my heart is knit
   To thine.

And now, dear Kate, we know, though late,
   Each mind.
Come, 'fore we part each hand and heart
   We'll bind.

THE
AMERICAN MELODIES.

PART II.

Songs composed at sea, comprising such melodies as were composed during my term of service in the United States Navy, in the years 1862 and 1863.

> " A life on the ocean wave,
>   A home on the rolling deep,
> Where the scattered waters rave,
>   And the winds their revels keep.
>
> " Like an ocean bird I pine
>   On this dull, unchanging shore:
> O give me the flashing brine,
>   And mad old Ocean's roar."
>
> —ANONYMOUS.

I PACED UPON THE QUARTER-DECK.

I paced upon the quarter-deck,
  And gazed far out upon the sea,
I warned the pilot at the wheel,
  Of every beacon light I'd see.
Cold was the night, the wind did blow,
  The waves dashed o'er the larboard side,
Atlantic's billows, crowned with foam,
  In fury with old Boreas vied.

But, worn with watching long and late,
  I heeded not the angry storm,
As every swell dashed o'er the ship,
  It chilled anew my shivering form ;
Although the Storm King reigned that night,
  And wrath and madness ruled the hour,
Made every spar and timber bend,
  In reverence to old Neptune's power.

'Twas not the howling winds I feared,
  Or plunging ship or surging sea,
For there I stood, unconscious of
  The dangers which environed me ;
But thinking of one I left,
  Who loved me, though so far away,
I do confess I wept at length—
  My tears mixed with the briny spray.

I wept and chided, like a child,
  The day when first I came to sea,
When I left loving Mary home,
  In solitude to weep for me.
O, how her anxious breast must feel—
  With what deep anguish must it burn,
As howls the storm around her door,
  For fear I never will return.

But when I've reached my destined port,
  If I should weather safe this gale,
With anchor weighed, and sails well spread,
  For home I'll hasten without fail.
When taking up the lengthened chain
  I trailed between my home and thee,
As link by link I near my love,
  I'll bless her for her constancy.

Off Hatteras, Dec. 7th, 1862.

THE MOON HAD JUST BOARDED ATLANTIC'S BROAD RIM.

The moon had ascended Atlantic's broad rim,
  And an ocean of silver presented to view,
The winds were at rest, and the stars glimmered dim,
  And our ship lay becalmed, for no breezes blew.

The sailor boy hied to his hammock for rest,
  To catch a few moments of peaceful repose,
But, weary, he scarcely his mattrass had press'd,
  When in slumbers truant mem'ry by visions arose.

Wide o'er the deep he looked back on the days
    When a child he reclined in his father's green bowers;
Again by Ohio the sailor boy strays,
    And on its gay banks he is culling wild flowers.

He watches young Jennie, his sister, at play,
    As now on the lily she rivets an eye,
Or, transported with rapture, she drops on the way
    Her gems, in pursuit of the gay butterfly.

The towering hill he ascends with delight—
    Surveys from its summit his fond home below;
Now transparent rivulets burst on his sight,
    As meandering through the green valleys they flow.

Thus dreaming unconsciously, time speeds away,
    While enjoying the haunts of his childhood awhile;
But midnight is past—'tis the dawning of day—
    And the sailor boy wakens to danger and toil.

Ah! mem'ry, thou fiend; how unwelcome to some,
    When we fancy we've drowned thee, with all of our care,
Alone in the still hours of midnight you come,
    And the breaking of morn finds us wrapt in despair.

WE LAID HER IN THE DARK BLUE SEA.

    We laid her in the dark blue sea,
      Its waters closed around her,
    I saw her as she sank from me,
      In ocean's shroud that bound her;
    Her face still bore the very smile
      That once did on it linger;
    I took, to loneliness beguile,
      The ring upon her finger.

That ring I have, that ring I'll keep—
　Close to my heart I'll place it;
When, thoughtless, she lies in the deep,
　I'll draw it forth and face it.
'Tis then I'll picture in my mind
　The lovely maid who wore it,
And fancy on its rim I'll find
　The tender hand that bore it.

Then shall her dark eye, raven hair,
　Rush in imagination,
Impress my heart, filled with despair,
　The deepest of sensation.
And when I see the surging brine
　By winds coaxed in commotion,
I'll think of her who does recline
　Beneath the Indian Ocean.

ADIEU, MY NATIVE LAND—A LONG ADIEU.*

Adieu, my native land—a long adieu!
　My gallant bark impatient waits for me;
And soon upon the ocean's boundless blue
　I'll turn my last and farewell look on thee.
Already weighing anchor in the bay,
　With full-swelled sails loud flapping in the blast,
She, proud, careens upon her distant way,
　With trembling timbers and with creaking mast.

She smoothly parts the waters with her prow,
　While gentle wavelets lap her starboard side,
Afar to seaward bears again; and now,
　Majestic, moves along in all her regal pride.

* On leaving New York, December 7, 1862.

The gentle breeze that sweels her snow-white sails
 Is filled with fragrance from some sunny isle,
While, slowly moving with the spicy gale,
 My noble craft glides lordly on the while.

But when again, land of the brave and free,
 Shall I return to stray each emerald bower,
Where often, in my former childish glee,
 I've wasted many a precious passing hour?
But fleeing time that, flying waits for naught,
 May yet bring fortune on his peerless wings,
When, laden with good tidings or with favors fraught,
 Of days again to saunter by thy springs.

FOR WEARY MILES THE SHIP HAD PLOWED.

 Tune—"*The Sky is Bright, the Breeze is Fair.*"
 For weary miles the ship had plowed
  Her onward progress through the sea,
 And left behind a track of foam,
  Which shone with diamond brilliancy.

 The royals to top-gallant mast
  With eager will embraced the breeze,
 While canvas swelled from ev'ry yard,
  From main-deck to the main cross-trees.

 The ensign proudly waved from peak,
  The pennant gaily from the main,
 Rejoicing in the rising breeze
  Which swept athwart the watery plain.

 The waters playing round her bow
  Would ever and anon retreat,
 But only to return again,
  Upon her oaken sides to beat.

THE
AMERICAN MELODIES.

PART III.

COMPRISING SUCH MELODIES AS WERE COMPOSED DURING THE
WAR FOR THE UNION.

> "The Union of lakes, the Union of lands,
> The Union that none can sever;
> The Union of hearts, the Union of hands,
> The American Union forever."
> —ANONYMOUS.

THE MINSTREL BOY HAS LEFT THE PLOW.

The minstrel boy has left the plow,
    No more he in the furrow sings;
Sweet nature's warbling songsters now
    No longer in his wild ear rings.
His home that once was in the glen
    Which skirts Ohio's tranquil stream,
Is now in camp of armed men,
    Where only swords and bayonets gleam.

Where once he saw the placid flood
    Of crystal streamlets purling by,
He now beholds the same in blood
    Roll past him in their purple dye.
But yet he loves his native land,
    For her he's left the woodland shade,
And marches with her patriot band
    To wield the deadly glist'ning blade.

His march is through wild Tennessee,
    Where army never trod before;
He braves the loud artillery
    And musketry's unceasing roar.
His bed is on the swampy ground,
    Amid the tall and treacherous grass,
With deadly rattlesnakes around—
    Where prowling alligators pass.

His sabre is the trusty one,
    His father used on Trenton's field,
Bequeathed to his worthy son,
    Which in his country's cause to wield.

4

How well he has applied that steel
Let Corinth and red Shiloh tell—
How many did its temper feel?
How many fighting 'neath it fell?

'TWAS NIGHT, AND WEARY I SANK TO REST.

TUNE—"*The Lake of the Dismal Swamp.*"

'Twas night, and, weary, I sank to rest,
  For the long day's march was done.
But scarcely had I the damp ground press'd,
When warlike dreams my mind distressed
  With battles we had lost and won.

Very often I thought I saw advance
  The enemy o'er across the field;
I caught the gleam of each shining lance—
I'd hear the steady and measured prance,
  As the cavalry charged and wheeled.

Again, I'd fancy our "lines" gave way—
  That our fate and cause were sealed;
I'd grasp my rifle without delay,
And spring from the ground whereon I lay,
  Till, awake, the delusion revealed.

Then, awake, I'd listen, but all in vain,
  For no sound fell on my ear,
Till, wrapt unconscious in slumber again,
In dreams I'd wander mid heaps of slain
  That was slaughtered far and near.

And now we routed the foe in turn,
　Though red was the field with blood;
And, as each patriot heart would burn
With terrible vengeance, all quarter spurn,
　As brave men only would.

Unbound, the iron dogs of hell
　Made gaps in everp rank,
While flew their screaming, screeching shell;
And, wheresoever their vengeance fell,
　The ground their red blood drank.

The air was filled with the rapid clash
　Of the deadly sabre blows,
Gallant was our cavalry dash;
While, raised aloft, would be seen to flash
　The sharp steel o'er our foes.

LAND OF THE BRAVE, LAND OF THE FREE.

　Land of the brave, land of the free,
　　Our Union ne'er shall fall,
　Since yonder ensign waved so proud
　　O'er Sumter's massive wall.

　It's bore the marks of many a fight,
　　Of many a stormy blast,
　Since Jasper climbed the tow'ring pole,
　　And nailed it to the mast.

　Then O, my God and country!
　　Shall traitors live?—and must
　They tread upon my nation's flag,
　　And trail it in the dust?

O, vengeance! give me here the sword
  To smite a treacherous friend;
Their rights I'll give, but never shall
  To such vile insult bend.

Woe! woe! upon each cursed foe,
  And blood shall be the cry,
Till every miscreant traitor's swept
  From 'neath our country's sky.

COME WHET THE DULL SWORD.

Come whet the dull sword, and the rifle make sure,
  And polish the old rusty gun,
We'll fight for a cause that is holy and pure,
  With a motto of "many in one."

We've sworn on our knees, when our forefathers died,
  To our colors to ever prove true,
And the last look they gave it was cast on their pride,
  Their pride of the red, white and blue.

That banner in triumph has waved o'er the seas,
  And ne'er in dishonor shall fall;
It has hailed the return of the morning's first breeze,
  As it fluttered and waved o'er the wall.

'Twas borne through the fight, on the red battle-field
  Where our ancestors perished and fell,
And while life remains, the sword we will wield,
  For the emblem we cherish so well.

All hail to thee, flag of my country—all hail!
  Many thousands may fall at thy shrine—
Aye! millions—and yet thy brave sons would not quail,
  Nor the cause of their country resign.

ALONE I TROD THE DEAD-STREWN WOODS.

Alone I trod the dead-strewn woods
  Which skirt the banks of Tennessee;
I thought of her, my former love,
  My Alice, ever dear to me.
And as I thought of her, far, far
  Away, so many leagues from here,
Expecting her no more to see,
  I wiped away a fallen tear.

'Tis not because I fear the foe,
  As yonder dead can testify,
Or that I fear the fatal shot,
  For I am not afraid to die.
But when I think that you, sweet maid,
  Will deeply mourn the loss you bore,
And that my death will grieve you so,
  It bleeds me to the bosom's core.

But when my country's foes are crushed,
  And peace assumes her welcome reign,
I'll ground my rifle for the time,
  And fold thee in these arms again.
Although I love you stronger still,
  And mourn your absence in my heart,
Yet, know, sweet maid, my country, too,
  At least should claim her legal part.

————

MY COUNTRY CALLS ME, I MUST HASTEN AND GO.

Farewell, home and friends, ye beloved of my bosom,
  To leave you the sorrowing tear feign must flow,
Your counsels and friendship regret I at losing,
  But my country calls me—I must hasten and go.

No wonder, dear mother, your tear-drops are falling,
    But leave you I must, for my country's foe
Doth threaten our fireside with sorrow and wailing,
    And my country calls me—I must hasten and go.

Thou pride of my heart, though your bosom is smarting,
    Most heavy, my darling, on you falls the blow,
But remember, my love, I must tell you, ere parting,
    That my country calls me—I must hasten and go.

Can I stand aloof from the cause which I cherish,
    When freedom's at stake, and my country? O, no!
I'll fly to the battle-field, though I should perish,
    For my country calls me—I must hasten and go.

THE SOLDIER'S DREAM.

Worn and wearied, I slept, on the cold ground reclining,
    With naught for my bed save a handful of hay;
The sky was unclouded, the stars dimly shining,
    And, dreaming, I dreamed of my friends far away.
I thought that once more I was back to my dwelling,
    That friends, wife and kindred stood smiling around,
And amusing the children with anecdotes telling,
    Of famed men and heroes in battle renowned.

Thus, blest with a vision of home and its pleasures,
    The hours glided by with their flight scarcely known;
But vain were the joys, and still vainer the treasures,
    As reason returns, they are vanished and flown.
But short was the while I was blest in my slumber
    With the happy and fond recollections of home;
The bugle's shrill notes soon aroused me in wonder,
    To hear the loud cry of "the foe come—they come."

OFT WHEN I TREAD MY LONELY BEAT.

TUNE—"*Our Flag is There.*"

Oft when I tread my lonely beat,
　My mind reverts, both night and day,
To home, and those connections sweet,
　Which I have left, far, far away.

Though many miles doth intervene
　'Twixt me and those I love so true,
Yet, in the midnight hour, I ween,
　Their well known lineaments I view.

But, say, fair silvery orb of light,
　Whose silvery face I love to see,
O, say—does Alice weep at night,
　And mourn in secret grief for me?

Does she not stray the silent vales,
　And long our parting hour deplore,
As in her agony she wails,
　Along Ohio's peaceful shore?

O, was I seated where thou art,
　High in the blue, arched heavens above,
I feign would from my orbit start,
　To press her to this breast of love.

MISCELLANEOUS POEMS.

IRELAND.

Respectfully inscribed to T. F. Meagher's Brigade, whose bravery and conspicuous gallantry, on the battle-fields of the New World, in the cause of American Independence, entitles it to the most sincere thanks, and lasting gratitude of every American heart.

O, Erin! land of chivalry and fame,
    Of patriot sons to freedom ever born,
Who've nobly battled in our country's name,
    And rushed to rescue in her hour forlorn;
For who like you, O, cherished "Isle of Green,"
    Came bravely forward, in the darkest hours,
And side by side thy Emerald flag was seen,
    In victory and triumph wave by ours.

Yes, nobly has thy gallant sons behaved,
    To save the Ark of Freedom from her foe;
For where our flag successfully has waved,
    They've truly aided in the crowning blow.
Then can Columbia forget what share
    Of true devotion by thy sons of toil?
Whose patriot blood is mingled with her own?
    Whose patriot bones lie bleaching on her soil?

O, no, "Green Isle!" O, no, thou "Emerald Gem!"
    Thy Corcoran and Meagher wreaths for thee
Have won; until that day of liberty dawns when
    You'll win new laurels, struggling to be free.
When, thinking o'er the past upon that day,
    America the avenging arm shall rise
To strike thy tyrants—all thy deeds repay,
    And plant the Tree of Freedom 'neath thy skies.

Thy consecrated sons to Freedom's shrine
  Can ne'er prove recreant to her holy cause,
Whate'er betides them in the course of time
  Still binds them closer to our equal laws.
Their blood is ever willing to be shed,
  They're always ready with a heroic arm,
They love to fill a patriot's gory bed,
  When shielding their loved equal rights from harm.

Columbia long shall cherish thee, fair Isle,
  In lasting honor of thy heroic dead,
And as upon their graves she weeps the while,
  She'll twine a hallowed wreath upon their bed.
Can she forget the sacrifice you've made,
  The noble bloods who've died in her defence?
No, no; her thousand Tones and Emmets* dead
  Shall cause her tears to flow through ages hence.

———

IOHN ADAMS'† LAMENT.

Respectfully dedicated to Henry Wallace Lynch, of the United States bark Brazilian.

My poor, down-trodden country, when
  Shalt thou lift up thy drooping head?
When shall thy soul of freedom wake,
  To strike the proud oppressor dead?

Where is the fire which flamed your sires—
  Made them forsake their native strand?
Was it to seek a foreign grave,
  A home to find in foreign land?

———

*Two well known martyrs to the cause of Liberty in Ireland.
† The well known patriot of Massachusetts, whose unflinching opposition to British tyranny and oppression made his name conspicuous in the annals of the Revolution.

No ; kneeling on a barren rock*
  When they had crossed Atlantic's wave,
They raised a song of praise to God,
  And swore they ne'er would live a slave.

And is this not your native land?
  And is this not their blessed sod?
Why will ye kneel to haughty kings,
  And bear their vile and cursed rod?

Then rise, my countrymen, arise!
  Shake off the shame of former years ;
Laugh at the tyrants when they treat,
  And wipe your eyes, and dry your tears.

Remember, oh ! remember, then,
  Each spot whereon your feet doth tread ;
For every inch, or foot, or rod,
  Was hallowed by your fathers' dead.

And will you view this lovely land
  By boasting tyrants lorded round?
O, wake, my countrymen, awake!
  Strike the oppressors to the ground !

LOVE AND FRIENDSHIP.

In this world there are many who call themselves friends—
They are friends while the favors of fortune extend ;
Then let it but blow in an opposite way,
When "I never did know such a one," they would say.

---

* Plymouth Rock, Massachusetts.

O, riches! what mighty allurements thou hast—
Alas! for the one who has treasure too vast;
The deceitful will follow, his friendship will own,
But when poverty strikes him their friendship is gone.

Such friendship, my friend, does exist not in you;
Your love it is purer, more constant and true;
To your friends be the same, and heed not fortune's blast,
But stand by, unsullied, a friend to the last.

OHIO.*

Along thy verdant banks I love to stray,
    And by thy crystal stream, Ohio, fair,
And hear the jovial thrush and robin's lay
    Warble resonant on the morning air.

O, who would not delight to rove along
    Thy halcyon waters, glassy, clear;
The first to hail the linnet's blythest song,
    Which greets at dawn the early riser's ear.

Yes; lovely are thy banks in autumn's morn,
    Yet lovelier far when spring does first return,
And spreads upon the bramble and the thorn
    The garb for which they now no longer yearn.

'Tis pleasant, too, just at the close of even',
    To feel the gentle zephyrs balmy blow,
And view the fast declining light of Heaven
    Flushed with that gorgeous golden, western glow.

---

*This river, meandering between the hills of Southern Ohio and Western Virginia, presents some of the most picturesque and lovely scenery imaginable. During the months of June, July and August the transparency of its waters is remarkable, winning for it the appellation of "La Belle Riviere," a title but justly bestowed.

I would not part thy wild, meandering stream
  For all the waters of the east or west,
For O, I love the bright, enamelled gleam
  Of sunset on thy crimson-purple breast.

ON THE DEATH OF WASHINGTON IRVING.

Columbia, the glory and pride of thy nation
  Has vanished, and left us but only his name ;
A star's disappeared from thy bright constellation,
  How pure was its lustre, how spotless its fame.

Though that star has descended, its fame is increasing,
  And brighter and brighter 'twill eternally burn ;
While the tears of his country shall fall without ceasing,
  To honor his mem'ry and hallow his urn.

Farewell, then, great Irving, unperishable, unfading
  Thy laurels shall be, though thy spirit has fled ;
Thy countrymen never shall be found evading
  The honor they owe the illustrious dead.

ON THE DEATH OF WILLIAM BETHEL.*

When nobles and monarchs have closed their career,
  There is many to write of their doom ;
But how few are the hearts for to sigh o'er their bier,
  And the tears that are shed on their tomb.

But thou, humble Bethel, I long will lament,
  Alas ! whom thy friend could not save ;
But as they pass by thee, with willing consent,
  They'll shed a sad tear on thy grave.

* Written at the request of a young lady on the death of her lover.

LINES ON THE OHIO.*

Respectfully inscribed to Miss Alice Gardner, of Quaker Bottom, Lawrence County, Ohio.

Roll on, fair stream ; Ohio roll
　Thy placid waters on their way ;
Green are the banks which hold your tide
　In meek submission to their sway.
Grand are the hills† which overlook
　The spreading "bottoms" far and wide,
Where bright appears each gentle brook
　That pours along its gentle tide.

Below the cotter's house appears
　Embosomed in ancestral trees,
From whence the country maiden's song
　Comes borne upon the gentle breeze.
And from the rip'ning fields of grain
　Is heard the merry laugh of glee—
The tasseled corn, with waving plumes,
　Rolls like the billows of the sea.

Then when the twilight's wed the day,
　And when is heard the lowering cow,
The rustic lads come signing home,
　The chattering blackbirds leave the plow.
The lark begins to seek her nest,
　Amid the meadows now so green ;
The noisy crows, above the trees,
　With sluggish flight are nowhere seen.

---

* Written in Rome township, Lawrence county, Ohio, July, 1860.
† I was standing on those truly "grand hills" when the above lines occurred to memory.

The swallow, which was all day long,
　A skimming o'er the river's breast,
Has sought the good old farmer's barn,
　And snugs securely in her nest.
Now from the hill the owl descends,
　And, perched upon the crumbling mill,
With doleful cries disturbs the vale,
　In concert with the whip-poor-will.

And now the frogs, from marsh and pond,
　With tireless throats, beguile the hour;
While countless fire-flies show their light
　Through every bramble, bush and bower.
The bat, with restless wing, is seen
　In rapid circles through the air,
As, darting on each insect thing,
　In haste obtains his nightly fare.

Now Luna, from the balmy east,
　Secures her throne, while not a cloud
Envelopes her fair, silvery face,
　Or soils her beauty with a shroud;
But, from her queenly seat on high,
　She smiles in silent grandeur down,
Adorns the landscape with her rays,
　And gilds the spires of yonder town.*

The fox, imprisoned in his cell,
　From whence he dare not now retire,
Lest Luna's light his steps betray,
　And guide the hunter's deadly fire.
The 'possum seeks secure retreat
　Amid the paw-paw's trackless growth,
Till, forced by hunger or by want,
　In search of food she sallies forth.

* Guyandotte, Virginia.

And now the moon's pale, slanting beams
Foretells another coming day;
While in the east the encroaching light
Disperse the stars before its sway.
Now silence reigns around supreme,
And hushed is the nocturnal fowl;
The morning calms the whip-poor-will,
And daylight rests the screeching owl.

BATTLE OF SOMERSET.*

I gazed, and lo! afar and near,
With hastening speed, now there, now here,
The horseman rode with glittering spear—
    'Twas awful to behold!

Ten thousand men, in dread array—
On every hill and mound they lay—
A dreadful sight it was that day
    To see the front they formed.

The polished sabres, waving high,
Flashed brightly in the morning sky;
While, beaming on dazzled eye,
    The glittering bayonets shone.

All, all was hushed among the trees,
Save now and then a gentle breeze,
Which stirr'd the brown and serried leaves
    That in the forest lay.

---

*The battle of Somerset (or Mill Spring, as it is more commonly called) was fought in Kentucky, between the rebel forces under Zollicoffer, and the Union forces under General Thomas. Here it was the former fell.

But what is that which greets mine eye?
Is it Columbia's sons I spy?
Hark! hark! I hear their battle cry—
    Their shouts of victory!

Still hotter does the conflict grow ;
While dealing death in every blow,
McCook charged on the routed foe
    His daring little band.

Rest, patriots, rest; the conflicts o'er,
Your erring brethren punished sore;
O, would they'd fight their friends no more,
    And cease this bloody strife.

SWEET MARY.

Sweet Mary, though I'm far away—
  Far from my peaceful home and thee—
Yet let not absence break the ray
  Of love that binds thy heart to me.
Though many long, long leagues divide
  Us, still I cannot think but you,
Though parted by our distance wide,
  In love is constant and is true.

Since last I saw thy form divine,
  Full many a month has passed away;
But is your love as strong as mine—
  As strong as mine, O, who can say?
I cannot say you love me not,
  And yet it does so often seem
That if I was not quite forgot,
  You'd wrote to me ere this, I ween.

But, Mary, should I judge you wrong—
  For who the heart's dark secrets know—
O, tell me if affection's strong
  As 't was in absent years ago.
Yet I'll remember, till I die,
  The day and hour when we did part;
The years may roll, the seasons fly,
  And still you hold enthralled my heart.

FAITH.

As points the needle which directs
  The ship upon the ocean's breast,
Until the mariner detects
  The distant port he's sailed in quest,
So Faith points to a port above,
  Where all is bliss without alloy;
It points, as on life's sea we rove,
  To that fair haven of endless joy.

HOPE.

As gleams the lonely beacon light
  Athwart the wild, tempestuous sea,
And shows the storm-tossed ship, at night,
  A harbor safe, whence she may flee,
So Hope, upon the sea of life,
  Will rise a beacon to the soul,
And guide us on, through danger, strife,—
  On safely to our destined goal.

CHARITY.

As dew is to the drooping flower,
  As rain is to the budding rose,
That, grateful for the needed shower,
  Their loveliest colors all disclose,
So Charity infuses joy,
  Distills its gifts on all around,
Which otherwise, for want, might die,
  And lose its sweetness in the ground.

LOVE.

What is true love? 'tis like the vine
  That winds around the sapling in the grove,
Or clings tenacious to the forest pine
  In fond embraces,—such is love;
And such is love—the fatal axe which fells
  The stately forest pine or sapling low,
Though every stroke upon the huge trunk tells.

SORROW.

The rose, beneath a burning sun,
  Will wither, pine and die,
The greenest spot on earth become
  A barren desert, dry.
So Sorrow will the true soul grieve,
  Oppress the fevered mind,
And on life's rosy pathway leave
  A barren waste behind.

DEATH.

And what is death ? 'tis but a transit from
  A transient life of misery to life
Eternal in the Heavens, where we'll come
  Into a heritage devoid of strife ;
It is the harbinger of happiness,
  The portal to another, better world,
A world immutable, of endless bliss,
  That never yet was to thy mind unfurled.

PERSEVERANCE.

Perseverance is a gift bequeathed from God,
  The only road to affluence and to fame,
And few that highway faithfully have trod,
  But what they've left a great, illustrious name.
If you, my friend, would tread it, make your mark ;
  Then to attain your object onward press,
Through fortune's smiles and bleak misfortunes dark,
  Remembering 'tis the true source of success.

FRIENDSHIP.

Like an oasis in the desert wide,
  A fertile spot upon a sandy plain,
Where, thirsty, famished travellers are supplied
  With what to them's most needful to obtain.
So Friendship, in this world of woe and care,
  Will fall like fragrance on the frozen heart,
To many who might otherwise despair,
  Its gifts of consolation will impart.

HUMILITY.

The humblest rose is not the least admired,
  Nor will it less attract the passer's eye
Because in gaudy colors unattired;
  The less with the most beautiful does vie.
So man, however humble will be seen,
  Whate'er his lot within this world may be,
Pride makes him but obnoxious to esteem;
  He's honored more for his humility.

INTEMPERANCE.

As the serpent, with some hidden wile,
  Will lure the bird to sure destruction on,
By some mysterious glance beguile
  The unsuspecting victim to its doom,
So will the luring glass attract the gaze,
  The treacherous cup, the poisoned bowl,
Until the senses wander in a maze,
  And sure destruction overtakes the soul.

INDEX.

PART I.